D0403267

THE MARK OF A W

★ Lightning bolt scar
   on forehead

★ Pretty good at Quidditch

★ Good at flying (not so
   good at Potions)

WIZARD WEAR

★ Three sets of plain robes (black)

★ Plain, pointed black hat for day wear

★ Protective gloves (dragon hide or similar)

★ Black winter coat with silver fastenings

REQUIRED READING

★ The Standard Book of Spells (Grade 1) by Miranda Goshawk

★ A History of Magic by Bathilda Bagshot

★ Magical Theory by Adalbert Waffling

PRIZEWINNING SPELLS

★ Wingardium Leviosa!

★ Alohomora!

NEVER GET CAUGHT WITHOUT YOUR...

* Wand
* Cauldron
* Telescope

Pets only a Gryffindor could love

- ★ Snowy owl
- ★ Rat
- ★ Dragon! (?)

EVERY GOOD WIZARD SHOULD GET...

★ Bertie Bott's Every Flavor Beans!
★ Chocolate Frogs!
★ Drooble's Best Blowing Gum!

No Wizard Can Have Enough...

★ Chocolate Frog
   Wizard Cards
★ Gold Galleons

THE HOUSES OF HOGWARTS

★ Gryffindor
★ Hufflepuff
★ Ravenclaw
★ Slytherin

GHOSTS OF HOGWARTS

★ Nearly Headless Nick
★ Bloody Baron
★ Peeves

Hogwarts' Most Magical Teachers Ever

★ Professor Dumbledore
★ Professor McGonagall
★ Professor Flitwick

HOGWARTS' OTHER TEACHERS

★ Professor Snape
★ Professor Quirrell

PETRIFICUS TOTALUS!

★ Filch
★ Mrs. Norris
★ Draco Malfoy

CREATURES TOO MAGICAL FOR WORDS

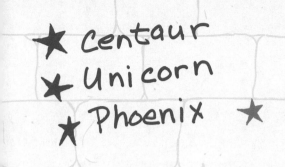

- ★ Centaur
- ★ Unicorn
- ★ Phoenix ★

CLASSES AT HOGWARTS

★ History of Magic
★ Charms
★ Transfiguration

QUIDDITCH GREATS

★ Oliver Wood
★ George Weasley
★ Fred Weasley

TEAMS WE LOVE TO BEAT!

- ★ Slytherin
- ★ Ravenclaw
- ★ Hufflepuff

HOLIDAY MAGIC!

★ A hundred fat roast turkeys

★ Flaming Christmas puddings

★ Silvery gray Invisibility Cloak

Muggles
(One Can't Avoid Them)

★ Uncle Vernon Dursley
★ Aunt Petunia Dursley
★ Dudley Dursley

HOW TO DRIVE A MUGGLE CRAZY

* Look as if you're having fun
* Pretend you're casting a spell
* Disappear onto platform nine
  and three-quarters

DECIDEDLY NONMAGICAL MOMENTS

★ Not knowing the answers in Snape's class

★ Falling off my broom ★

STUFF THAT'S AGAINST THE RULES AT HOGWARTS

★ Going into the Forbidden Forest

★ Dragons

★ Magic between classes

HOGWARTS FOREVER!
(SOME FAVORITE MEMORIES)

★ Playing on the Quidditch team for Gryffindor

★ The end-of-the-year feast

BIG SECRETS!

- ★ The restricted section of the library
- ★ Where the Sorcerer's Stone is hidden

SECRET WISHES
(IN THE MIRROR OF ERISED)

- ★ Being with my parents (me)
- ★ Winning the Quidditch Cup (Ron)
- ★ Woolen socks (Dumbledore)

SUBLIME DESSERTS

★ Treacle tarts!

Shopping Fit For A Sorcerer

★ The Leaky Cauldron
★ Eeylops Owl Emporium
★ Ollivander's ★

SCARY STUFF

★ Climbing the Tower with Norbert

★ Riding through the forest on Firenze

★ Getting past Fluffy

FUN STUFF

★ Sneaking around
   in my Invisibility Cloak

★ My Nimbus Two Thousand

WHAT I'M GOING TO DO THIS SUMMER

* ★ Go home to the Dursleys (ugh)
* ★ Visit Ron and the Weasleys (YES!)

MY DREAMS FOR THE NEXT MAGICAL YEAR AT HOGWARTS